The Frogs Wore Red Suspenders

RHYMES BY **JACK PRELUTSKY**

The Frogs

Wore Red Suspenders

PICTURES BY **PETRA MATHERS**

SCHOLASTIC INC.
New York Toronto London Auckland Sydney
Mexico City New Delhi Hong Kong Buenos Aires

ISBN 0-439-56058-6

Text copyright © 2002 by Jack Prelutsky.
Illustrations copyright © 2002 by Petra Mathers. All rights reserved.
Published by Scholastic Inc., 557 Broadway, New York, NY 10012,
by arrangement with Greenwillow Books, an imprint of
HarperCollins Publishers. SCHOLASTIC and associated logos
are trademarks and/or registered trademarks of Scholastic Inc.

12 11 10 9 8 7 6 5 4 3 2   3 4 5 6 7 8/0

Printed in the U.S.A.   08

First Scholastic printing, September 2003

Watercolors were used for the full-color art.

The text type is Cochin.

In memory
of Garth Williams
—J. P.

For Till and Brenda,
who are the bee's knees
—P. M.

CONTENTS

THE FROGS WORE RED SUSPENDERS

The frogs wore red suspenders
and the pigs wore purple vests,
as they sang to all the chickens
and the ducks upon their nests.

They croaked and oinked a serenade,
the ducks and chickens sighed,
then laid enormous spangled eggs,
and quacked and clucked with pride.

IN THE HEART OF SOUTH DAKOTA

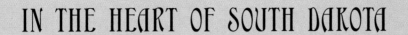

In the heart of South Dakota,
Jenny Jay stepped off a train,
leapt upon a nearby bison,
raced across the windy plain.

On that day in South Dakota,
Jenny Jay sat on a fence,
gazing at the wondrous mountain
topped with giant presidents.

CARPENTER, CARPENTER

Carpenter, carpenter, build us a house,
a sweet little house for a mouse and a spouse,
a mouse and a spouse and a family too,
we know that you can, and we hope that you do.

Build it of brick so it's cozy and warm,
to keep us from harm in a cold winter storm.
As soon as you finish, we'll pay you with cheese,
carpenter, carpenter, build our house, please.

WINNIE APPLETON

Out of bed hopped Winnie Appleton,
bounced a ball upon the floor,
bounced and bounced it through the hallway,
down the stairs, and out the door.

Through the streets of Minneapolis,
Winnie Appleton bounced that ball,
bounced and bounced it on the sidewalk,
bounced and bounced it off a wall.

Winnie Appleton crossed the river,
on the bridge she bounced that ball,
bounced and bounced it all that morning
till she finally reached St. Paul.

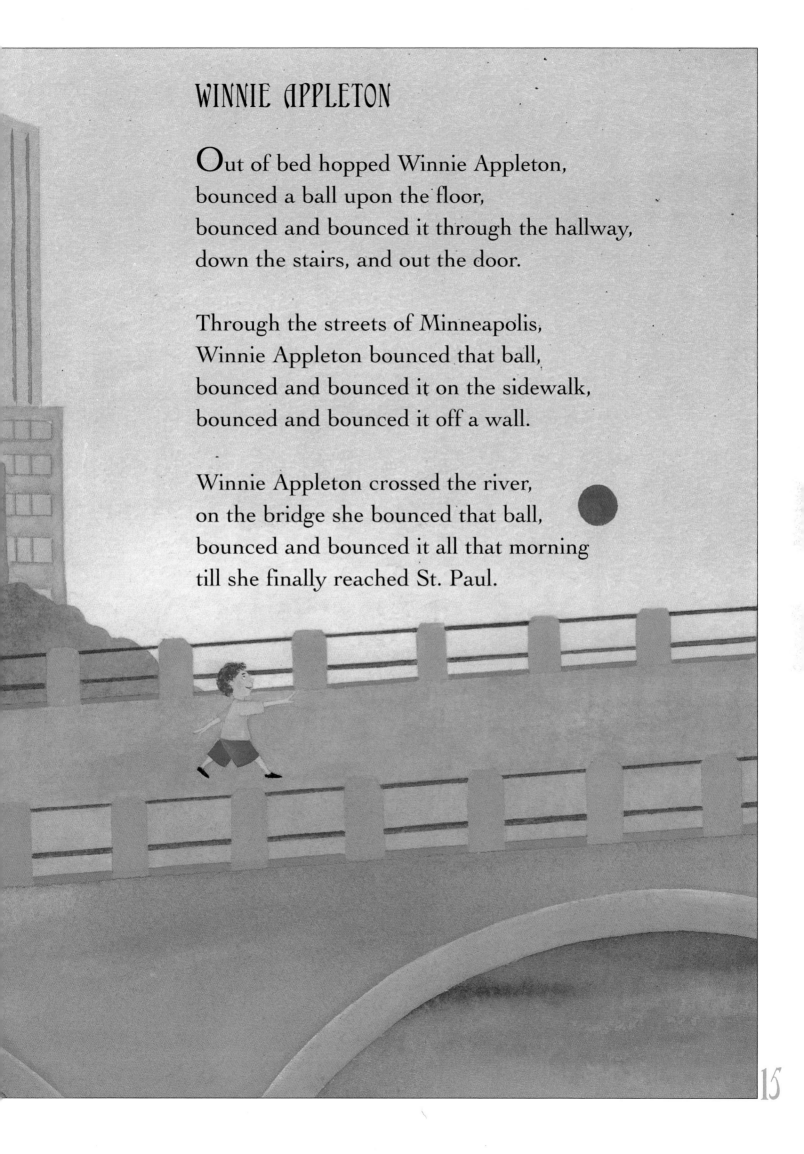

IN A WINTER MEADOW

In a winter meadow
icy breezes blow,
snowshoe hares are running
softly through the snow.

Up and down they scurry,
darting left and right,
snowshoe hares are running,
dressed in winter white.

PEANUT PEG AND PEANUT PETE

Peanut Peg and Peanut Pete,
on a bright Atlanta street,
call in voices loud and clear,
"Peanuts! Get your peanuts here!"

"Peanut cookies, peanut cakes,
peanut butter, peanut shakes,
peanut ices, peanut pies,
peanut sauce, and peanut fries!"

All day long they gaily sell
peanuts still inside the shell,
peanuts salty, peanuts sweet—
Peanut Peg and Peanut Pete.

SPOTTER AND SWATTER

Spotter and Swatter,
two talented otters,
crack mussels and clams
on their bellies all day.

They swallow down dozens,
then play with their cousins,
and chase one another
through Monterey Bay.

THERE WAS A TINY BAKER

There was a tiny baker
who had a tiny shop,
he baked a tiny cookie
with frosting on the top.

He snatched it from the oven
and ate that cookie up,
then washed it down with sarsaparilla
from a tiny cup.

IN INDIANAPOLIS

In Indianapolis, what did we see?
An elephant perched on a sycamore tree,
sipping warm milk through an oversize straw—
In Indianapolis, that's what we saw.

In Indianapolis, what did we do?
We danced on the green with a blue kangaroo.
The elephant sneezed, so we ran off and hid—
In Indianapolis, that's what we did.

RED HORSE, WHITE HORSE, BLACK HORSE, GRAY

Red horse, white horse, black horse, gray,
in a pasture, hard at play,
snort and neigh and stamp their feet,
nibble bluegrass, fresh and sweet.

Through the fields they romp and race,
frolicking with speed and grace,
on a fair Kentucky day . . .
Red horse, white horse, black horse, gray.

I WENT TO THE STORE

I went to the store
for a pear and a plum.
The fruit was all gone,
so they sold me a drum.
I asked them for butter,
they offered me glue.
I tried to buy bread,
but they sold me a shoe.

They sold me a lamp
when I tried to buy cheese.
Instead of potatoes,
I wound up with keys.
They didn't have milk,
so they sold me an oar —
I'll never go back
to that store anymore.

GRANNY GOODING

Granny Gooding lost her footing,
fell into a pudding vat.
There was pudding on her jacket,
pudding, pudding in her hat.

There was pudding in her slippers,
pudding, pudding on her dress.
Ever since she lost her footing,
Granny Gooding's been a mess.

IN WINNEMUCCA

In Winnemucca, way out west,
a monkey sat in a bluebird's nest.
The bluebird squawked and fussed all day,
Till the monkey ran to San Jose.

SARAH SMALL

In her garden, Sarah Small
grows galoshes, short and tall.
Shirts of yellow, hats of red
beautify her flower bed.

Near pajamas, row on row,
multicolored sweaters grow.
Neckties flutter in the breeze
underneath the mitten trees.

Shoes of every shape and size
blossom right before her eyes.
Stocking vines adorn the wall,
planted there by Sarah Small.

ONE OLD OWL

One old owl upon a tree,
high atop a hill,
watched the forest silently
while the night was still.

One old owl looked around,
while the moon was bright,
flapped its wings without a sound
and flew into the night.

BARNABY BOONE

Barnaby Boone, in his yellow balloon,
flew from El Paso one bright afternoon.
He drifted for days through the blue Texas skies,
feasting on hamburgers, hot dogs, and pies.

He drifted up north, and he drifted out east,
until he had finished the last of his feast.
He ran out of food, so he came back to earth,
landing his yellow balloon in Fort Worth.

WELCOME

I'M A LITTLE BROWN TOAD

I'm a little brown toad,
and I live all alone,
I hop hop hop
from stone to stone.

I have a happy grin
as I hop down the road,
for I'm glad glad glad
I'm a little brown toad.

ONE DAY IN SEATTLE

One day in Seattle
I sat by the Sound.
The salmon were jumping,
the birds flew around.
The seagulls were begging
for morsels of bread,
as ominous clouds
gathered high overhead.

A ferry went out,
and a ferry came in.
It started to rain,
I got soaked to my skin.
Seattle is lovely,
but I cannot lie—
without an umbrella
it's hard to stay dry.

42

IN THE TOWN OF TUCUMCARI

In the town of Tucumcari,
Teeny Dobbs and Tiny Grand
hopped atop a lizard's back
and headed south across the sand.

They were noisy, they were merry,
till they reached the town of Hobbs.
There the lizard bucked and tossed them—
Tiny Grand and Teeny Dobbs.

BABY IN A HIGH CHAIR

Baby in a high chair,
baby in a bib,
baby in a stroller,
baby in a crib.

Baby with the giggles,
baby with a smile,
such a lovely baby,
happy all the while.

IN TUSCALOOSA

In Tuscaloosa, after dark,
the donkeys gathered in the park.
The ducks and chickens came along,
and an old-time band played an old-time song.

There were pigs and cows in the green grass field,
and the cows all mooed, and the pigs all squealed,
and the ducks quack-quacked, and the donkeys brayed,
and the chickens clucked as the music played.

They danced a jig and they danced a reel,
then they all sat down to a fine hot meal
of corn and okra, dumpling stew,
at that Alabama barbecue.

EVERY MORNING IN FORT MYERS

Every morning in Fort Myers,
on the Gulf of Mexico,
there's a flock of puzzled penguins
looking high and looking low.

All along the beach they waddle,
searching for a sign of snow —
they won't find it in Fort Myers,
on the Gulf of Mexico.

TOMMY LOST A PENNY

Tommy lost a penny,
a nickel, and a dime,
Tommy lost his shiny watch
and does not know the time.

Tommy found his penny,
his nickel, and his dime.
His watch is in a magpie's nest
and keeping perfect time.

IN MINOT, NORTH DAKOTA

In Minot, North Dakota,
three mice went out to play.
They bundled up in snowsuits
one cold December day.
They wrestled and they tumbled,
they made a fort of snow,
as temperatures grew colder,
and winds began to blow.

They built a handsome snowmouse,
about four inches high.
They'd barely put the nose on
when snowflakes filled the sky.
A wind came out of nowhere,
their snowmouse blew away,
and so they built a bigger one
that North Dakota day.

FURRY FURRY SQUIRREL

Furry furry squirrel,
hurry hurry hop,
scurry up the tree trunk
to the very top.

When you reach the branches,
hurry turn around.
Furry furry squirrel,
scurry to the ground.

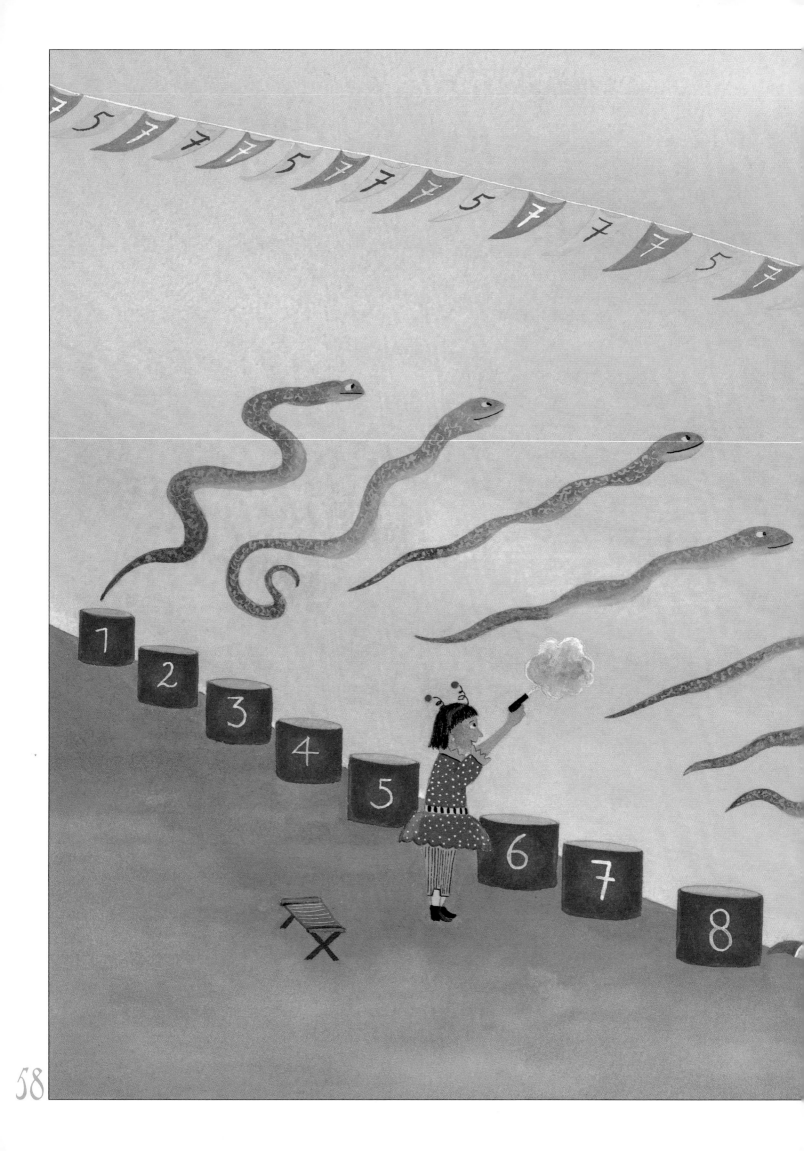

SEVEN SNAILS AND SEVEN SNAKES

Seven snails and seven snakes
swam around the five Great Lakes.
They took seven years to go
from Thunder Bay to Buffalo.

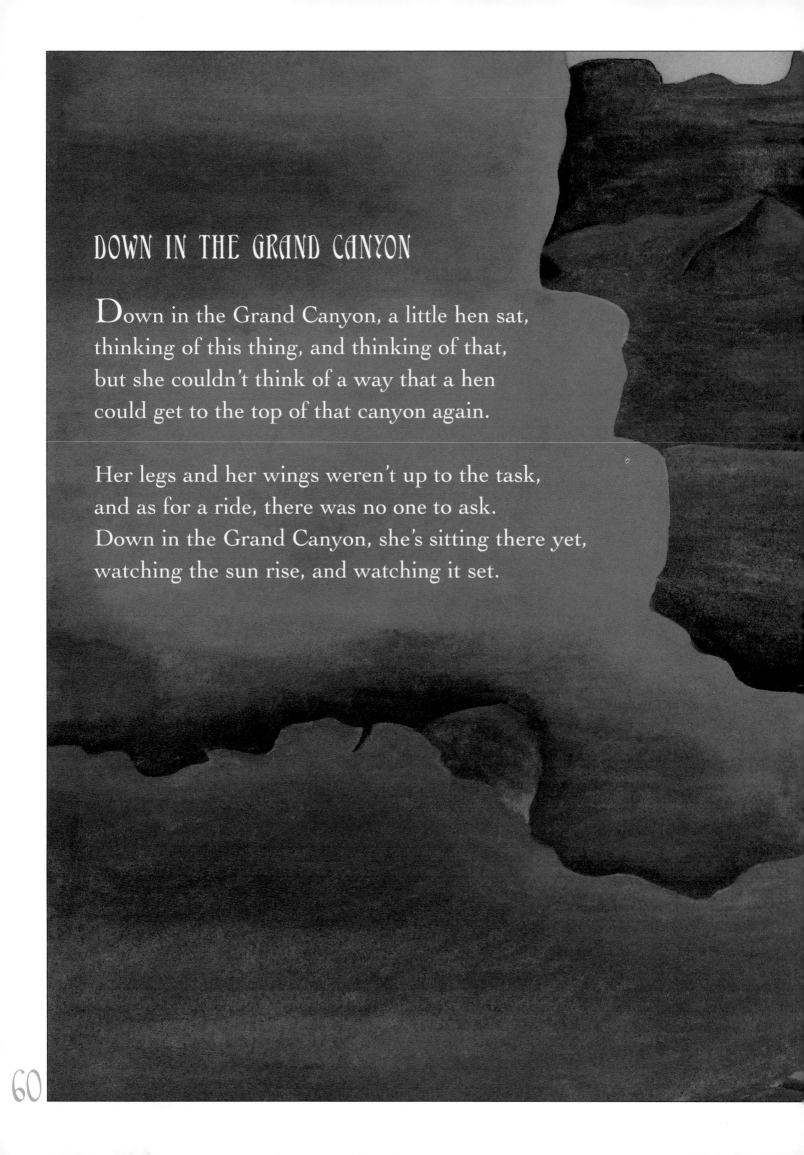

DOWN IN THE GRAND CANYON

Down in the Grand Canyon, a little hen sat,
thinking of this thing, and thinking of that,
but she couldn't think of a way that a hen
could get to the top of that canyon again.

Her legs and her wings weren't up to the task,
and as for a ride, there was no one to ask.
Down in the Grand Canyon, she's sitting there yet,
watching the sun rise, and watching it set.

TEN BROWN BEARS

Ten brown bears with big bow ties
gobbled plates of apple pies,
and with every pie they ate,
they piled up an empty plate.

When they had a ten-foot pile,
they arose in single file,
and with bellies fat and fed,
ten brown bears marched home to bed.

Jack Prelutsky's poems are recited, laughed over, and memorized by children across the country. His inventive wordplay and unpredictable rhymes have appeared in such favorites as *The New Kid on the Block*, *Something Big Has Been Here*, *A Pizza the Size of the Sun*, and *It's Raining Pigs & Noodles*. For younger readers his work includes two companions to this book: *Ride a Purple Pelican* and *Beneath a Blue Umbrella*, both illustrated by Garth Williams; several books illustrated by Peter Sís, including *The Dragons Are Singing Tonight*; and *Awful Ogre's Awful Day*, illustrated by Paul O. Zelinsky.

Petra Mathers has written and illustrated many books for children, most recently her very popular "Lottie's World" series.

She lives with her husband, Michael, beside the mighty Columbia River in Oregon.